VANISHING CHAINS

Vanishing Chains

DERICK CHIBILU

THE CHRISTIAN BLOGGER

| 1 |

Copyright

| 2 |

Book Description:

In "Vanishing Chains," immerse yourself in the riveting journey of a group of inmates as they meticulously orchestrate an audacious escape from the confines of a maximum-security prison. Navigating treacherous alliances, deciphering cryptic clues, and constantly evading the ever-watchful eye of the relentless warden, the line between freedom and captivity blurs in the shadows of incarceration.

Throughout this gripping narrative, the intricate plan unfolds with each passing event, revealing unexpected twists and subjecting the characters to high-stakes moments. The prison walls, once an impenetrable fortress, now serve as the backdrop for an elaborate dance of deception, where the boundaries between ally and adversary become increasingly blurred.

Will this resilient group of inmates overcome the formidable odds stacked against them and successfully vanish from the chains that bind them, or will the consequences of their daring escape catch up with them, casting shadows over their fleeting taste of freedom? "Vanishing Chains" is not merely a thriller; it's an exploration of the indomitable human spirit, tested in the crucible of confinement. The narrative immerses you in a world where determination, cunning, and the relentless pursuit of freedom serve as guiding lights in the darkest corners of the prison complex.

As the intricate plot continues to unfold, the characters find themselves navigating the labyrinth of their elaborate escape plan, encountering unforeseen challenges and unexpected alliances. The thrill intensifies as the consequences of their actions reverberate within the cold, unforgiving walls of the prison.

"Vanishing Chains" invites you to witness a tale that transcends the boundaries of incarceration, exploring the limits of human determination and the lengths one is willing to go to break free. Will their daring escape be the ultimate triumph, or will the shadow of captivity linger, casting doubt on the fragile nature of their newfound liberty?

In the sequel to "Vanishing Chains," the narrative takes a sharp turn as the protagonist's grapple with the complexities of life beyond the prison confines. Each chapter unfolds a different facet of their struggle to adapt as they face the challenges of reintegrating into society. From building new alliances to confronting old enemies, the characters find themselves in a world that is both liberating and unforgiving. As they navigate the intricacies of freedom, the novel explores the psychological toll of their past actions and the constant threat of being pulled back into a life they thought they left behind. "Unraveling Threads" is a gripping exploration of the aftermath of escape, where the real test of resilience begins.

| 3 |

"The Perfect Plan Unfolds"

In the heart of Stonehaven Penitentiary, where steel bars echoed with the weight of lost dreams, an intricate escape plan quietly took shape. James Harper, a man with a mind as sharp as the prison bars surrounding him, became the mastermind behind a daring plot that would challenge the very foundations of the maximum-security facility.

In a dimly lit cell, James, with his keen intellect and determination, formulates the blueprint for what he believes could be the perfect escape. Through meticulous observation and discreet conversations, he assembles a team of individuals whose unique skills and backgrounds will be crucial for success.

As James unveils the initial stages of his plan, we are introduced to the key players: Marcus "Shadow" Rodriguez, a former locksmith with a checkered past; Emily "Whisper" White, a cunning and resourceful inmate known for her ability to move in the shadows; and Thomas "Silencer" Turner, a once highly regarded computer hacker now serving time for cybercrimes.

The events explore the harsh realities of prison life, setting the stage for the desperation that fuels the characters' determination to break free. As the characters develop their roles in this intricate dance of deception, individuals are left on the edge of their seats, eager to witness how the perfect plan will unfold and what challenges lie ahead.

With the foundation laid, the subsequent events promise a gripping journey through alliances and betrayals, the unraveling of cryptic clues, and the relentless pursuit of freedom against all odds. "Vanishing Chains" is poised to be a thrilling escape adventure that delves into the complexities of human nature and the pursuit of liberty in the face of seemingly insurmountable barriers.

| 4 |

"Behind Enemy Lines: Infiltrating the Prison"

As night settled over Stonehaven Penitentiary, a cloak of shadows descended upon the cold, imposing walls. The air thickened with tension as the carefully selected team of escape artists prepared to put their plan into motion. James Harper, the architect of the daring escape, knew that success depended on infiltrating the prison's inner workings.

The unfolding events commence with the team assembling in the dimly lit confines of their shared cell. James briefs them on the first crucial step: acquiring insider information. Marcus "Shadow" Rodriguez, a man with a knack for blending into the darkness, becomes the key player in this phase. His past experience as a locksmith provides him with unique access to areas beyond the usual inmate boundaries.

James instructs Marcus to discreetly gather intel on the prison's layout, guard routines, and any vulnerabilities that could be exploited. The events skillfully navigate through Marcus's covert missions, highlighting the cat-and-mouse game he plays with the security apparatus. The audience is taken into the underbelly of the prison as Marcus navigates the labyrinth of corridors and hidden passages, capturing the essence of the high-stakes infiltration.

Meanwhile, Emily "Whisper" White employs her cunning skills to eavesdrop on conversations among guards and other inmates. Through subtle interactions and clever maneuvers, she begins to piece together the puzzle of the prison's inner workings. The tension rises as the team works in tandem, aware that a single misstep could spell disaster for their meticulously planned escape.

Thomas "Silencer" Turner, the computer hacker, plays a crucial role in accessing the prison's electronic systems. His fingers dance across the keyboard in the dead of night, by-passing security protocols and leaving no digital trace. The events build suspense as Silencer uncovers hidden vulnerabil-ities, opening doors that were thought to be impenetrable.

"Behind Enemy Lines" sets the stage for the unfolding drama, showcasing the team's determination to overcome the formidable obstacles within the prison walls. The seg-ment concludes with a sense of anticipation, hinting at the challenges and revelations that await in the subsequent stages of the elaborate escape plan.

| 5 |

"Alliances and Betrayals in Cell Block C"

Within the confines of Cell Block C, where alliances were as fleeting as the prison shadows, James Harper's plan faced its first true test. The unfolding events transpire against the backdrop of the claustrophobic cells and echoing footsteps of the guards, revealing the delicate dance of alliances and potential betrayals that could make or break the intricate escape scheme.

James gathers his team in the secluded corner of their shared cell, the air heavy with a mixture of anticipation and distrust. Marcus "Shadow" Rodriguez, fresh from his reconnaissance missions, presents the gathered intelligence on guard rotations, blind spots, and potential weaknesses in the prison's security. The stakes rise as the team realizes the gravity of the challenges ahead.

As the group navigates the delicate web of relationships in

Cell Block C, alliances form based on mutual survival instincts and shared desperation for freedom. The events explore the dynamics between the inmates, each harboring their motives and fears. Friendships are forged in the crucible of confinement, and the audience witnesses the delicate balance of trust and skepticism that characterizes life behind bars.

Emily "Whisper" White uses her charm and cunning to cultivate crucial connections within the prison's social hierarchy. Through covert conversations and strategic interactions, she identifies potential allies among the inmates and even manages to glean information from unsuspecting guards. However, the ever-present threat of betrayal looms, as hidden agendas and conflicting interests threaten to unravel the fragile bonds.

In this segment, you are introduced to the enigmatic figures of Cell Block C, each with a story of desperation and a desire for liberation. The events skillfully navigate the complexities of human nature, painting a vivid picture of the alliances that emerge under the looming specter of incarceration.

As the unfolding events progress, tension escalates, and the team grapples with the realization that trust is a fragile commodity within the prison's unforgiving walls. "Alliances and Betrayals in Cell Block C" sets the stage for the psychological intricacies that will shape the course of the escape plan, leaving the audience on the edge of their seat, eager to discover the next twist in this gripping tale of survival and treachery.

| 6 |

"The Cryptic Clues of the Prison Underground"

In the dimly lit recesses beneath Stonehaven Penitentiary, a labyrinth of forgotten passages and hidden tunnels transforms into the next battleground for James Harper's escape plan. The unfolding events take place against the backdrop of the prison's mysterious underground, where ancient secrets and cryptic clues hold the keys to unlocking freedom.

James, Marcus, Emily, and Thomas gather in their secluded corner, meticulously examining the intelligence gathered from their prior endeavors. Marcus's reconnaissance had uncovered a network of forgotten tunnels, concealed beneath layers of neglect and disuse. The team recognizes that navigating this subterranean maze could be their ticket to eluding the watchful eyes above ground.

Skillfully exploring the team's journey into the underground, where every step is shadowed by the oppressive weight of the prison's history, the air thickens with the scent of dampness, and the echo of distant footsteps adds an eerie rhythm to their progress. As they venture deeper, cryptic symbols etched into the walls hint at a hidden history waiting to be unraveled.

The team deciphers these symbols, exposing a complex network of interconnected tunnels and concealed passages. The unfolding events carry a sense of discovery, as each clue propels them further into the clandestine depths of the prison's substructure. Along the way, they encounter remnants of forgotten escape attempts and the echoes of desperate whispers from inmates long gone.

Emily's keen observational skills prove invaluable as she interprets the meaning behind the cryptic symbols, unveiling the intricate web of tunnels crisscrossing beneath the prison. The events capture the team's growing realization that this subterranean journey is not only a physical passage but a metaphorical descent into the complexities of their motivations and the mysteries enveloping Stonehaven.

"The Cryptic Clues of the Prison Underground" sets the stage for the team's descent into the heart of the prison's secrets, where every step forward brings them closer to both liberation and the unknown challenges that lie ahead. As this segment concludes, anticipation lingers on the precipice, ready to unravel the next layer of this elaborate escape plan.

| **7** |

"The Key maker's Dilemma"

Descending deeper into the labyrinthine passages beneath Stonehaven Penitentiary, the team confronted an unexpected challenge that would strain the limits of their ingenuity—the necessity for a master key to unlock the final barriers to freedom. In the heart of the underground maze, the intricate dance of strategy and risk unfolded, revealing the daunting obstacle known as "The Keymaker's Dilemma."

James Harper, the strategist orchestrating the escape, faced the stark reality that their journey through the cryptic tunnels had led them to a sealed door, impervious to their collective skills. Marcus "Shadow" Rodriguez, the locksmith, now confronted the formidable task of fashioning a master key capable of opening the final barriers obstructing their path to freedom.

Exploring Marcus's internal struggle became a focal point

as he grappled with the weight of this responsibility. The damp walls of the underground tunnel served as the backdrop to tense moments, with Marcus examining the door, pondering the delicate balance between precision and speed. The team's fate hung in the balance as he crafted makeshift tools necessary for the challenging task ahead.

The narrative skillfully traversed Marcus's meticulous process, underscoring the challenges of forging a key without arousing suspicion. The ever-present threat of discovery and the consequences of failure added a layer of suspense, infusing the underground chamber with a palpable sense of urgency.

Meanwhile, Emily "Whisper" White and Thomas "Silencer" Turner, leveraging their unique skills, contributed to the team's efforts. Emily maintained vigilant watch, her eyes scanning the shadows for signs of approaching danger, while Thomas ensured their digital tracks remained concealed, preventing the security systems from detecting their presence.

"The Keymaker's Dilemma" delved into the complexities of trust within the team as Marcus grappled with doubts about his ability to deliver the key without compromising their plan. The narrative unfolded with a series of twists, revealing unexpected challenges and decisions that would determine the fate of the escape.

As this segment concluded, the anticipation lingered, leaving the audience on the edge, wondering whether Marcus's skills would prove sufficient to surmount "The Keymaker's Dilemma" and unlock the path to the next stage of the elaborate escape plan.

| 8 |

"Countdown to Chaos: Stirring the Inmates"

With the key in hand, crafted with a precision born of desperation, the team faced a new challenge in their escape plan's next phase. In the heart of Stonehaven Penitentiary, James Harper orchestrated a calculated disruption to divert attention away from their impending breakout. The events unfold against the backdrop of "Countdown to Chaos: Stirring the Inmates."

As the team gathered in their secret meeting place beneath the prison, the air was charged with anticipation. James outlined the need for a carefully orchestrated disturbance within the inmate population, a strategic maneuver to draw the focus of both guards and surveillance away from their planned escape route. The stakes were high, and the success of their plan depended on the chaos that would ensue.

The events skillfully navigate the team's efforts to stir the inmates into a controlled frenzy. Emily "Whisper" White, with her innate ability to influence and manipulate, took charge of spreading carefully crafted rumors among the prisoner ranks. Marcus "Shadow" Rodriguez moved like a wraith through the cell blocks, subtly sowing discontent and fanning the flames of resentment that simmered beneath the surface.

In the dimly lit corridors, Thomas "Silencer" Turner utilized his digital prowess to disrupt the prison's communication systems, ensuring that the chaos remained unpredictable and resistant to immediate control. The countdown to the orchestrated mayhem began, each moment ratcheting up the tension as the team awaited the critical point where distraction and confusion would provide cover for their escape.

The events unfold with a blend of suspense and strategic maneuvering, capturing the intricate dance between the team members and the volatile reactions of the inmate population. The segment explores the delicate balance between controlled chaos and the potential for the situation to spiral out of hand, threatening not only the success of the escape plan but the safety of everyone involved.

As "Countdown to Chaos" progresses, individuals are drawn into the escalating turmoil, left to ponder the consequences of the team's calculated gamble. The stage is set for the explosive moments that will determine the success or failure of their elaborate escape plan, creating a sense of anticipation that permeates the pages of this gripping segment.

| 9 |

"The Warden's Watchful Eye"

Amidst the orchestrated chaos within the confines of Stonehaven Penitentiary, a watchful eye loomed large over the unfolding events. In the segment titled "The Warden's Watchful Eye," James Harper and his team navigated the delicate dance of evading the prison's highest authority, whose keen intuition and watchful gaze posed a constant threat to their meticulously planned escape.

As the chaos stirred by the team's strategic maneuvers reached its crescendo, Warden Malcolm Covington found himself at the epicenter of a prison in turmoil. Events unfold with glimpses into the warden's perspective, revealing his calculated response to the unrest within the penitentiary walls. Covington, a figure of authority with a reputation for cunning, sensed that something more than a mere inmate scuffle was afoot.

James Harper, ever cognizant of the warden's watchful eye, led his team through the shadows, utilizing the diversion to their advantage. The segment delves into the psychological chess match between Harper and Covington, two minds each plotting their moves with the high-stakes game of escape as the ultimate prize.

As the team maneuvered through the labyrinthine corridors, Marcus "Shadow" Rodriguez employed his expertise to avoid the surveillance cameras that dotted the prison landscape. Emily "Whisper" White strategically blended into the chaos, diverting attention from the real motives behind the orchestrated disturbances. Thomas "Silencer" Turner worked diligently to maintain a digital cloak, shielding the team's movements from the prying eyes of the prison's security systems.

The segment skillfully builds tension as the warden's suspicions deepen, his every decision and action affecting the delicate balance of the escape plan. The players are drawn into the cat-and-mouse game between the team and the warden, each move carrying the weight of potential discovery and failure.

"The Warden's Watchful Eye" sets the stage for the escalating conflict between the escapees and the prison's highest authority, leaving you on the edge of your seat as you anticipate the unfolding consequences of this high-stakes game of evasion and pursuit. The segment is a masterful interplay of strategy, suspense, and the ever-present threat of exposure in the face of the watchful eye of authority.

| 10 |

"Silent Shadows: Navigating the Night Shift"

As the chaos ignited by the calculated disturbance continued to reverberate through Stonehaven Penitentiary, James Harper and his team pressed forward under the shroud of night. In the segment titled "Silent Shadows: Navigating the Night Shift," events unfold in the eerie quietude of darkness, where the team faced the challenges of eluding the heightened vigilance of the night shift guards.

The segment opens with the prison plunged into nocturnal stillness, broken only by the distant echoes of unrest that lingered in the corridors. James, Marcus, Emily, and Thomas moved in tandem, their steps guided by a meticulous plan to exploit the vulnerabilities presented by the cover of night. The team's journey through the shadowy recesses of the prison became a ballet of stealth and precision.

Marcus "Shadow" Rodriguez, living up to his moniker,

took point as the group's silent guide through the dimly lit passages. The segment skillfully weaves through the challenges of navigating the labyrinthine prison structure in darkness, emphasizing Marcus's expertise in exploiting blind spots and avoiding the surveillance of the night shift guards.

Emily "Whisper" White played a crucial role in maintaining the team's covert approach. With a keen awareness of the soundscape around them, she ensured that their movements were masked by the natural symphony of the night. The segment explores the heightened senses of the team members as they silently tread through the prison's corridors, acutely aware that a single misplaced footfall could spell disaster.

Thomas "Silencer" Turner utilized his digital skills to manipulate the security systems further, ensuring that their movements went unnoticed by the electronic eyes that patrolled the prison. The night shift guards, burdened by the weariness of their late-hour duties, became unwitting accomplices in the team's journey toward freedom.

"Silent Shadows: Navigating the Night Shift" captures the delicate balance of tension and poise as the team advances toward the final stages of their escape. Individuals are immersed in the atmosphere of quiet suspense, where every breath, every step, holds the potential for both success and peril. As the segment concludes, the team remains poised on the precipice of the unknown, with the night their ally and the shadows their sanctuary.

| 11 |

"The Unexpected Turn of the Guard"

As the team navigated the intricate dance of silence and shadows, an unforeseen twist unfolded in the clandestine corridors of Stonehaven Penitentiary. Titled "The Unexpected Turn of the Guard," this segment takes an unforeseen detour, introducing a pivotal moment that challenges the team's resolve and adds an unexpected layer of complexity to their escape plan.

The segment opens with the team cautiously advancing through the dimly lit passages, their senses heightened by the ever-present awareness of potential threats. However, the unexpected turn of events occurs when a routine shift change among the guards takes an unforeseen detour. A veteran guard, Officer Robert Shaw, renowned for his perceptiveness and strict adherence to protocol, takes an unscheduled route that intersects with the team's escape path.

James Harper, the strategist, quickly assesses the situation. The team, concealed in the shadows, watches as Officer Shaw, unknowingly deviating from the usual route, approaches their location. The tension rises as the team grapples with the dilemma of whether to alter their course or risk an encounter that could jeopardize the entire escape plan.

Marcus "Shadow" Rodriguez, with his expertise in stealth, becomes the linchpin in this unexpected encounter. The segment skillfully navigates the team's decision-making process as they weigh the potential consequences of altering their carefully crafted plan. The shadows become both ally and adversary, as the team contemplates whether to wait in the darkness or take a bold and unpredictable course of action.

Emily "Whisper" White, with her ability to influence and manipulate, finds herself in a position to divert Officer Shaw's attention. The segment explores the delicate dance between distraction and concealment, highlighting the team's adaptability in the face of the unforeseen.

"The Unexpected Turn of the Guard" introduces an element of unpredictability, adding a layer of suspense to the escape plan. As the team grapples with this unanticipated challenge, they are drawn deeper into the intricacies of the plot, wondering how this unforeseen twist will shape the course of their desperate bid for freedom. The segment leaves them on the edge of anticipation, eager to unravel the consequences of this unexpected encounter in the shadowy corridors of Stonehaven Penitentiary.

| 12 |

"Cat and Mouse: Evading the Pursuers"

Following the unexpected encounter with Officer Robert Shaw, the escape team found themselves in a high-stakes game of pursuit and evasion. In the intense maneuvering of "Cat and Mouse: Evading the Pursuers," the escapees navigate the prison's corridors while being relentlessly pursued by both the watchful guards and the unforeseen consequences of their actions.

Their journey kicks off with the team swiftly shifting from the shadows, propelled into a heart-pounding race against time. James Harper, the strategist, adjusts the plan on the fly, using every ounce of his ingenuity to outmaneuver the relentless pursuers. The prison's alarms echo through the corridors, signaling the heightened state of alert as the pursuit intensifies.

Leading the charge, Marcus "Shadow" Rodriguez pushes

his expertise in evasion to its limits. The sequence skillfully captures the suspense as the team employs every trick in their arsenal, from doubling back through hidden passages to exploiting blind spots created by the chaos they've sown. Immersed in the urgency of the escape, the experience resonates with the team's quickening heartbeat with each step.

Officer Shaw, now aware of the breach in protocol, becomes a formidable adversary in the cat-and-mouse chase. The sequence weaves between the perspectives of the pursuers and the pursued, creating a dynamic interplay of strategy and desperation. Emily "Whisper" White, with her gift for diversion, orchestrates distractions to mislead the guards, adding an additional layer of complexity to the unfolding drama.

Thomas "Silencer" Turner ensures their digital tracks remain obfuscated, leading the pursuers on a circuitous path of confusion. The prison's surveillance systems become both a tool for evasion and a constant threat as the team navigates the labyrinthine corridors, seeking the elusive exit that promises freedom.

"Cat and Mouse: Evading the Pursuers" is a pulsating experience of tension, where every corner turned and every decision made carries the weight of potential capture. Engaged in the relentless pursuit, the audience shares the adrenaline-fueled experience of the escape team as they grapple with the consequences of their calculated actions. As the pursuit reaches its zenith, the sequence leaves observers at the precipice of uncertainty, eagerly anticipating the next twist in this intricate and daring escape plan.

| 13 |

"Crossing the Line: Freedom or Recapture?"

As the escape team raced against the relentless pursuit within the depths of Stonehaven Penitentiary, "Crossing the Line: Freedom or Recapture?" delves into the pivotal moment where the line between liberation and captivity teeters on a razor's edge.

The episode begins with the team reaching a crucial juncture, standing on the narrow threshold between the prison's oppressive confines and the tantalizing promise of freedom beyond. James Harper, the architect of their audacious escape, must make split-second decisions that will determine the fate of everyone involved. The team's breathless pause accentuates the weight of the choices ahead.

Marcus "Shadow" Rodriguez, Emily "Whisper" White, and Thomas "Silencer" Turner stand at the precipice, their eyes fixed on the potential escape route. The episode skillfully captures the internal struggle of each character, torn between the allure of freedom and the ever-present threat of recapture. The echoes of pursuing footsteps and distant alarms add palpable urgency to the decision they must make.

Tension mounts as Officer Robert Shaw closes in, his determination matched only by the resolve of the escapees. The episode weaves between perspectives, immersing observers in the psychological struggle as the team grapples with the consequences of crossing the line into the unknown. The episode unfolds with a sense of inevitability, capturing the emotional turmoil as the team takes the decisive step. Every footfall becomes a heartbeat, resonating with the uncertainty of their chosen path. Observers are carried through a visceral experience, feeling the rush of wind and the weight of anticipation as the escape team plunges into the uncharted territory beyond the prison walls.

"Crossing the Line: Freedom or Recapture?" sets the stage for the climactic moments that will shape the destiny of the escapees. The episode leaves observers on the edge of their seat, questioning the outcomes of this daring decision and eagerly awaiting the resolution of the intricate and elaborate escape plan that has unfolded across the preceding episodes.

| 14 |

"Reckoning: Confrontation at the Prison Gates"

In the gripping conclusion of this captivating tale, titled "Reckoning: Confrontation at the Prison Gates," the culmination of the escape plan unfolds against the stark backdrop of the prison gates. As the escape team breaches the threshold between captivity and freedom, the story navigates the high-stakes confrontation that will determine the ultimate success or failure of their audacious endeavor.

The episode opens with the escapees emerging from the shadows, blinking against the blinding light of the outside world. The cool night air carries both the scent of newfound liberty and the lingering tension of the pursuit. James Harper, Marcus "Shadow" Rodriguez, Emily "Whisper" White, and Thomas "Silencer" Turner stand united at the prison gates, their collective gaze fixed on the unknown expanse that lies beyond.

As the escape team braces for the final reckoning, Officer Robert Shaw and the prison authorities close in, determined to quash the insurrection that has unfolded within their walls. The story skillfully weaves between perspectives, capturing the contrasting emotions of the pursuers and the pursued. Observers are thrust into the heart of the confrontation, feeling the palpable tension that permeates the air.

James Harper, the mastermind behind the elaborate escape plan, faces Officer Shaw in a battle of wits and determination. The dialogue crackles with intensity as the two adversaries engage in a verbal sparring match, each aware of the significance of this final reckoning. The escape team, their resolve unwavering, stands united against the looming threat of recapture.

Marcus, Emily, and Thomas, each bearing the weight of their roles in the escape plan, confront the consequences of their choices. The story captures the emotional complexity of the moment, from the triumph of overcoming the prison's oppressive grip to the uncertainty that accompanies the journey into the unknown.

"Reckoning: Confrontation at the Prison Gates" is a crescendo of tension and resolution, where the threads of the intricate escape plan are woven together. The episode delivers the final moments of suspense, revelation, and the ultimate judgment that awaits the escape team. As the prison gates swing open or closed, observers are left with a sense of closure, marking the end of a thrilling saga that unfolded within the confines of Stonehaven Penitentiary.

"Into the Unknown: Life Beyond the Prison Walls"

In the shadowed expanse beyond the prison walls, Marcus "Shadow" Rodriguez ventured cautiously into the crisp night air, a taste of freedom both invigorating and daunting. The moonlight unveiled a world distinct from Marcus's prison-bound reality, with distant city lights serving as reminders of the life he once took for granted. The hum of traffic and the night air's scent mingled in a blend of liberation and uncertainty.

Alongside him, figures emerged from the shadows—James Harper, the mastermind, Emily "Whisper" White, and Thomas "Silencer" Turner. Their eyes adjusted to the new-found freedom as the trio, united by a shared escape goal, exchanged silent glances conveying volumes. Their meticulously crafted escape plan, developed during countless nights in their cells, was set in motion.

Adrenaline surged as the trio contemplated the challenges ahead. The city skyline promised a distant liberation, but the path was fraught with peril; the prison was a formidable fortress. Their first foray into the unknown led them to a discreet rendezvous point, avoiding detection. A waiting silhouette marked their contact, the key to the next phase of their audacious plan. The journey teemed with uncertainty, requiring forged alliances and outsmarted enemies.

Moving with the determined caution of those acquainted only with captivity, the quartet left behind the chains of imprisonment, yet the echoes of their past lingered. Each step away from the prison walls marked a dance with fate, secrets concealed in the night. The intricacies of their escape unfolded, exposing the challenges of navigating a nearly forgotten world. "Into the Unknown" unveiled the suspenseful journey of James, Marcus, Emily, and Thomas as they ventured into a life beyond prison, where freedom demanded their utmost wit and resilience.

| 15 |

"Forging New Identities: Ghosts in Plain Sight"

Within the rhythm of the city's pulse, James, Marcus, Emily, and Thomas ventured into the urban labyrinth, their faces veiled in the anonymity of shadows. The escape plan required more than just liberation from the prison's physical confines—it demanded a metamorphosis into entities unrecognized and unseen in this new world.

The quartet arrived at a dimly lit establishment nestled in the heart of the city's underbelly—a refuge for those dwelling on the fringes of society. Here, amidst the mingling scents of desperation and opportunity, they initiated the process of crafting new identities. Entering a concealed room at the rear, a contact awaited their arrival.

"Power lies in names," the contact declared, a mysterious figure whose features remained obscured by the dim light.

"In this realm, you're nobody until you morph into some-body else."

The room transformed into a covert workshop, papers strewn about, and identities waiting to be born. James, Marcus, Emily, and Thomas discarded their prison personas like discarded skins, embracing the challenge of assuming new roles. Forged documents and altered histories lay before them—the instruments of their metamorphosis.

Emily, meticulous in her attention to detail, fine-tuned the information on counterfeit passports, while Thomas, the technologist, ensured their digital traces evaporated into the void. Marcus, the locksmith, undertook the creation of physical disguises that would render them unrecognizable to both allies and adversaries, while James closely inspected every document.

As they toiled, the quartet engaged in discussions about the significance of seamlessly blending into the city's bustling tapestry. Their new identities transcended mere names on documents; they served as the means of survival in a world oblivious to their past. Conversations navigated the subtleties of maintaining a discreet presence, avoiding scrutiny, and mastering the art of existing as phantoms in plain view.

The unfolding scenario detailed the intricate process of shedding one's identity and embracing a new persona, exploring the hurdles of fading into invisibility within a society eager to classify and delineate. "Forging New Identities" established the groundwork for a story where the characters' survival hinged on their capacity to transform into shadows in a world indifferent to their true selves.

"Strangers in a Strange Land: Navigating the Outside World"

From the vantage point of an onlooker, James, Marcus, Emily, and Thomas emerged from the concealed workshop, ready to navigate the vibrant city with their newly assumed identities. As they stepped into the urban flow, they presented themselves as unfamiliar figures in a realm that felt both foreign and liberating.

The city sprawled before them, an intricate landscape of possibilities and pitfalls. The quartet moved through the crowded streets with a watchful eye, recognizing every interaction as a potential risk. Each step through the city's arteries allowed them to feel the pulse of life and the weight of their newfound freedom.

The escape plan required more than just manipulated

documents; it demanded an intimate understanding of the social landscape they now occupied. The quartet observed the daily rhythm, seamlessly blending into the city's flow. They frequented inconspicuous cafes and parks, engaging in conversations with coded language to evade prying ears.

In this unfamiliar terrain, the characters encountered both allies and potential threats. Evading law enforcement's gaze was not the only challenge; deciphering the unspoken rules of the streets proved equally crucial. The unfolding scenario explored the subtleties of survival—choosing the right alleys, interpreting the unspoken signals of fellow inhabitants, and mastering the art of fading into the background.

As they navigated the uncharted territory, each member of the quartet faced individual challenges. James, the mastermind, felt lost in a new city. Marcus, accustomed to the rigid routines of prison life, grappled with the overwhelming choices of the external world. Emily, relying on acute instincts, discerned hidden dangers beneath the surface. Thomas, the technologist, adapted his skills to manipulate the digital shadows, ensuring their presence remained elusive.

The unfolding drama captured the tension of being strangers in a landscape that could be both forgiving and unforgiving. Every encounter, every decision, represented a step into the unknown. Their journey aimed not only to escape the past but also to find a place in a world that had progressed without them.

| 17 |

"The Double-Edged Freedom: Choices and Consequences"

Against the backdrop of the city's rhythm, James, Marcus, Emily, and Thomas found themselves standing at the crossroads of their new lives. The freedom they sought was a complex proposition, offering liberation while also requiring decisions with repercussions that reverberated through the fabric of their existence.

Navigating the urban sprawl with a practiced ease born out of necessity, the quartet confronted decisions that would mold their futures. Each step they took was a calculated risk, and every alliance they formed carried the potential for betrayal. The unfolding scenario revealed the intricacies of the choices ahead, exposing the delicate equilibrium between survival and the pursuit of a life beyond the prison walls.

Haunted by shadows of his past, James, the mastermind, wrestled with the question of how he was going to live his life looking over his shoulders for the rest of his life. Marcus grappled with the ethical dilemmas posed by their escape. Each decision became a moral compass, forcing him to confront the fine line between right and wrong in their quest for freedom. Emily, the strategist, foresaw the consequences of their actions, her mind weaving through a labyrinth of potential outcomes. Thomas, the technologist, delved into the digital realm, where choices resonated with tangible repercussions.

The city, with its neon-lit streets and concealed corners, transformed into a playground where their decisions rippled like waves in a pond. Maintaining anonymity while establishing crucial connections for the next phases of their escape plan became their challenge. Every handshake, every whispered conversation, held the potential to shape their destiny.

As the characters moved through this unfolding scenario, observers were immersed in the complexity of their interpersonal dynamics. The alliances forged were strategic yet fragile, with the consequences of a misstep looming like a specter. The unfolding situation explored the tension between the desire for absolute freedom and the recognition that every choice carried its own burden.

"The Double-Edged Freedom" laid the foundation for a tale where the characters grappled not only with external threats but also with internal conflicts arising from the choices they made. As the repercussions of their actions began to manifest, the scenario hinted at the ever-present question: Would their pursuit of freedom lead to redemption, or would it further entangle them in the intricate web of consequences?

| 18 |

"Shattered Reflections: Confronting the Past"

Bathed in the neon glow of the cityscape, James, Marcus, Emily, and Thomas stood at a crossroads where the burdens of their past clashed with the uncertain promise of the future. In the chapter titled "Shattered Reflections," the four grappled with the specters they had sought to escape, compelled to confront the fragments of their former lives.

The unfolding scenario plunged into the characters' histories, laying bare the fractured reflections of a past that continued to cast shadows over their present. James, the mastermind, felt like he had lost his grip on life. Marcus, haunted by the errors that led to his incarceration, revisited the choices that defined his existence. Emily, the enigmatic whisper among them, faced the scars of betrayal and loss etched into her very being. Thomas, the once high-profile hacker, confronted the repercussions of a digital life that had unraveled.

The city, now a canvas painted with shattered memories, became a stage for their internal struggles. Familiar places were revisited, with each alley and street corner silently witnessing the chapters they wished to erase. Amidst the urban chaos, they grappled with the realization that true freedom demanded more than escaping physical confines—it required liberation from the chains of remorse and regret.

As they confronted their pasts, the characters unearthed hidden truths and confronted the emotional wreckage beneath the surface. The scenario explored the impact of their actions on their relationships, laying bare vulnerabilities and fostering a deeper understanding of the bonds that held them together.

In "Shattered Reflections," the city served as a metaphorical mirror reflecting not only the external challenges of their escape plan but also the internal conflicts shaping their journey. The chapter paved the way for a poignant exploration of redemption, forgiveness, and the transformative power of confronting one's own demons. Standing at the crossroads of past and present, observers were invited to witness the unfolding drama of personal reckoning, adding intricate layers to the tapestry of the escape plan.

| 19 |

"Underground Alliances: Building a New Network"

The city's darker side transformed into a covert arena for James, Marcus, Emily, and Thomas as they immersed themselves in the intricate craft of forming alliances within the shadows. In the installment titled "Underground Alliances," the trio encountered the task of constructing a network of contacts whose allegiances remained concealed from the vigilant gaze of law enforcement.

The unfolding scenario commenced with the trio navigating dimly lit alleys and discreet meeting spots, exchanging coded messages with contacts shrouded in anonymity. The city's rhythm resonated with the hushed tones of conversations, a symphony of secrets guiding their escape plan.

Marcus, pragmatic in his approach, sought out individuals whose skills complemented their strengths. The locksmith reached into the hidden realm of the underground, connecting with craftsmen whose expertise spanned from forging documents to establishing concealed safe houses. Emily, astutely perceptive, identified potential allies whose motivations aligned with their own, ensuring that alliances were founded on shared objectives.

Thomas, leveraging his digital expertise, established a covert network transcending physical boundaries. The dark web and encrypted communication channels served as the infrastructure for their clandestine operations, forming a virtual maze where information flowed securely.

As the characters engaged in the surreptitious dance of trust and deception, observers were introduced to a cast of figures with mysterious pasts and concealed agendas. Each alliance posed a dual threat, offering resources while holding the potential for betrayal. The scenario unfolded the intricate negotiations, the tacit alliances, and the bonds forged in the crucible of shared secrets.

The unfolding situation hinted at the complexity of the underground network, revealing the layers of intrigue beneath the surface. The city, with its concealed enclaves and winding alleys, became the playground where the characters tested the limits of trust and loyalty.

"Underground Alliances" laid the groundwork for a tale in which the evolution of the escape plan was not solely driven by the characters' physical actions but also by the alliances they cultivated within the shadows. As the network expanded, so did the stakes, promising both salvation and peril as the four delved deeper into the intricate web they themselves had woven.

| 20 |

"The Hidden Enemy: Old Threats in a New Setting"

In the heart of the city's labyrinth, where shadows clung to the edges of every alley, James, Marcus, Emily, and Thomas discovered that the past was an unrelenting specter. "The Hidden Enemy" unfolded as they encountered familiar faces and unearthed old threats that had followed them into the tangled expanse of their newfound freedom.

As they navigated the city's underbelly, they became aware that the echoes of their past had not faded. A figure emerged from the shadows, a face they had hoped to leave behind within the prison walls. The hidden enemy, once thought defeated, resurfaced with a thirst for retribution.

The narrative delved into the tension of facing an adversary they had underestimated—the remnants of a former life that had come back to haunt them. James, Marcus, Emily, and Thomas found themselves entangled in a cat-and-mouse game, their escape plan suddenly under threat from an un-expected source.

The hidden enemy operated in the shadows, exploiting vulnerabilities and preying on their fears. The chapter unveiled the psychological warfare waged against them, with taunting messages and cryptic threats that hinted at a deeper conspiracy. As the characters grappled with the resurgence of an old nemesis, they were drawn into the suspense of unraveling mysteries, and the stakes escalated to a dangerous level.

The city, once a canvas for their escape plan, became a battleground where alliances were tested, and they had to confront the consequences of past actions. The hidden enemy, like a ghost from the prison's past, forced them to re-evaluate loyalties and question the very foundations of their escape.

"The Hidden Enemy" set the stage for a narrative that wove together the complexities of personal history and external threats. As they faced a familiar foe in an unfamiliar setting, the chapter hinted at the intricate interplay between past and present, adding a layer of suspense that would shape the trajectory of their escape plan.

| 21 |

"A Taste of Normalcy: Adjusting to Life Outside"

The city's cadence mellowed as James, Marcus, Emily, and Thomas cautiously entered the domain of a life they had nearly forgotten—one that mirrored normalcy. In "A Taste of Normalcy," the four confronted the task of assimilating into the fabric of daily life, adopting routines that concealed the intricacies of their escape plan.

The unfolding situation depicted scenes of the characters attempting to grasp the threads of ordinary life. James slowly started to assimilate in daily routines. Marcus, previously bound by the structured routines of prison, found solace in the simplicity of commonplace activities—grocery shopping, navigating public transport, and engaging with strangers in everyday settings. Emily, wielding her enigmatic charm, aimed to establish connections extending beyond the confines of the escape plan, weaving the fabric of a life that approached normalcy.

Thomas, the technologist, wrestled with the sensory overload of a world he had only known through digital interfaces. The city's sights, sounds, and textures became a labyrinth of new experiences. As the characters adapted to the rhythm of life outside, the unfolding scenario explored the duality of their existence—the delicate equilibrium between the yearning for normalcy and the ever-present shadow of their elaborate escape plan.

Through their interactions with everyday people, observers witnessed the juxtaposition of the mundane and the extraordinary. The unfolding situation delved into the emotions of rediscovering the taste of freedom, even as the characters-maintained vigilance, cognizant that the illusion of normalcy could crumble at any moment.

The city itself assumed a character role in this scenario, its streets and parks offering glimpses of a world where the pursuit of a taste of normalcy was fraught with challenges. The unfolding scenario painted a portrait of a delicate dance between the desire for a life unburdened by the past and the relentless pull of the escape plan.

"A Taste of Normalcy" laid the groundwork for the characters to grapple with the paradox of yearning for a life that felt ordinary while being tethered to the extraordinary circumstances defining their existence. As they navigated the subtle nuances of normalcy, the unfolding scenario hinted at the fragility of their newfound equilibrium and the impending storm lurking on the horizon of their escape plan.

"Behind Closed Doors: Secrets and Complications"

In the hidden corners of the lives they had adopted, James, Marcus, Emily, and Thomas encountered the revelation that secrets and complications awaited behind closed doors. The unfolding scenario of "Behind Closed Doors" portrayed the characters wrestling with the dichotomy of the lives they led, where the pursuit of freedom collided with the intricacies of personal relationships and the concealed layers of their elaborate escape plan.

The scenario initiated with glimpses of the four striving to establish a semblance of normalcy in their daily routines —rented apartments, stable employment, and interactions with neighbors oblivious to their pasts. However, within the refuge of their private spaces, the characters confronted the gravity of the secrets they harbored.

Motivated by the necessity to safeguard those he cherished, James, with his keen intellect, yearned for opportunities to unleash his mental skills. Marcus found himself ensnared in a complex web of half-truths and evasions. Emily, shrouded in mystery, navigated the delicate equilibrium between forming authentic connections and upholding the barriers shielding her secrets. Thomas, the technologist, wrestled with the repercussions of a digital breadcrumb trail threatening to unveil their escape plan.

As the characters grappled with the complications of their dual lives, the unfolding situation delved into the nuanced interplay of trust and deception. "Behind Closed Doors" explored the emotional toll of concealing the truth from those in their inner circle, alluding to the strains that secrecy imposed on their relationships.

The city, with its expansive neighborhoods and intimate spaces, provided a backdrop for the characters to contend with the intricacies of their covert existence. The unfolding scenario suggested the fragility of the facades they had erected, as well as the potential unraveling of meticulously crafted plans.

While the quartet navigated through secrets and complications, they were immersed in a scenario blurring the boundaries between loyalty and self-preservation. The unfolding situation established the platform for the characters to face the personal consequences of their escape plan, where each closed door harbored the potential for revelation, and every secret carried the weight of repercussions capable of reshaping the trajectory of their journey.

| 23 |

"Echoes of the Past: The Haunting of Freedom"

In the midst of their newfound lives, James, Marcus, Emily, and Thomas found that the echoes of the past reverberated in the corners of their existence. "Echoes of the Past" unfolded as they faced unexpected reminders of the life they had fought to leave behind, the haunting specters threatening to shatter the fragile illusion of freedom they had crafted.

The chapter began with Marcus catching a glimpse of a face from his past in a crowded market—a former associate, a figure believed to be safely left behind within the prison walls. Emily sensed the subtle shifts in the air, the telltale signs of a presence she thought she had eluded. Thomas, through encrypted messages and cryptic emails, discovered that the digital shadows of their past were not as dormant as they had hoped.

As the characters confronted these echoes, the narrative

explored the psychological toll of a past that refused to fade away. The city, once a canvas for their escape plan, now became a maze of uncertainty, with every street corner and anonymous face carrying the potential to unravel the carefully constructed threads of their new lives.

They grappled with the realization that true freedom might forever be haunted by the shadows of the past. The chapter delved into the psychological landscape of fear and paranoia, as the characters questioned the boundaries between reality and the lingering remnants of the life they had sought to escape.

"Echoes of the Past" set the stage for a narrative that blended suspense with introspection, where the characters faced the challenge of reconciling their desire for a clean break with the inescapable echoes of the lives they had left behind. As they navigated the haunting of their freedom, they were drawn into the increasing complexity of the escape plan, where the past threatened to become an indelible part of their uncertain future.

| 24 |

"A Dangerous Reunion: Crossing Paths with the Past"

In the intricate maze of the city, James, Marcus, Emily, and Thomas found themselves on an unforeseen collision course with their past in "A Dangerous Reunion: Crossing Paths with the Past." As they maneuvered through the bustling streets and concealed alleys, a perilous reunion unfolded, threatening to unveil the carefully guarded secrets of their escape plan.

The unfolding situation commenced with Marcus participating in what appeared to be an unremarkable gathering, only to discover the reappearance of a face from his history—a reunion far from coincidental. Emily, finely attuned to her intuition, sensed impending danger in the atmosphere, her instincts forewarning her of a reunion carrying more menace than nostalgia. Thomas, the technologist, uncovered digital clues hinting at a convergence of old alliances and new threats.

As the characters became entangled in this perilous reunion, the unfolding scenario explored the complexities of relationships forged in the crucible of shared history. The city, once a backdrop for escape, now transformed into a stage for the clash of past and present. Every step, every glance, bore the weight of unspoken history.

The situation unfolded as a dance of cryptic conversations and concealed motives, where alliances faced scrutiny, and hidden agendas came to light. James, Marcus, Emily, and Thomas grappled with the challenge of maintaining the secrecy of their escape plan while confronting the specters they had aimed to leave behind.

"A Dangerous Reunion" established the groundwork for a scenario that fused suspense with the emotional intricacies of confronting one's past. As the characters confronted the dangers of intersecting with old alliances, they were drawn into a tense and intricate dance, where the distinction between friend and foe blurred, and the escape plan encountered its most precarious moments. The unfolding scenario hinted at escalating stakes, promising an exhilarating climax where the past and present would collide in a perilous dance of fate.

| 25 |

"Unraveling Threads: The Web of New Challenges"

In the intricate interweaving of their escape plan, James, Marcus, Emily, and Thomas found themselves ensnared in unforeseen challenges, each thread leading to a fresh revelation and a heightened sense of urgency. "Unraveling Threads" played out as they faced a web of complexities that jeopardized the carefully woven fabric of their freedom.

The unfolding scenario commenced with James, Marcus, Emily, and Thomas dissecting the aftermath of the perilous reunion. Secrets were exposed, alliances underwent scrutiny, and the city's pulse quickened with an undercurrent of tension. They recognized that their escape plan had evolved into a fragile web, susceptible to the unpredictable forces of the world they endeavored to navigate.

As they traversed the intricate threads of their challenges, the unfolding scenario delved into the multifaceted nature of the obstacles they encountered. The city, once a canvas for escape, morphed into a labyrinth of uncertainty, each alley and street corner presenting a new challenge. They grappled not only with external threats but also with internal conflicts, as the strains on their relationships became more pronounced.

The unfolding scenario revealed the emergence of a new adversary, one whose motivations remained elusive and whose influence extended into the hidden recesses of their lives. The characters confronted the reality that their escape plan was not a linear journey but a dynamic process, continually evolving and adapting to the twists and turns of their circumstances.

"Unraveling Threads" laid the groundwork for a climax where the characters would be compelled to face the repercussions of their choices. As the challenges intensified, the escape plan took on a life of its own, demanding resilience, adaptability, and a reassessment of their initial objectives.

The unfolding scenario hinted at the unpredictable nature of their journey, leaving observers on the edge of anticipation as James, Marcus, Emily, and Thomas found themselves entangled in the intricate web of new challenges, where the unraveling threads of their escape plan promised both danger and revelation.

| 26 |

"The Liberation Symphony"

In the culmination of their tumultuous journey, James, Marcus, Emily, and Thomas stood at the precipice of a new beginning. The threads of their escape plan, once delicate and unpredictable, now wove a tapestry of resilience and transformation. As they faced the ultimate reckoning, the cityscape bore witness to their metamorphosis.

The challenges, intricacies, and alliances forged in the crucible of their escape plan converged into a moment of profound clarity. The labyrinth of uncertainties they navigated became a testament to the indomitable human spirit and the unwavering pursuit of freedom.

The echoes of their past actions lingered, but the trio stood resilient, having confronted not only external adversaries but also the shadows within. The city, once a backdrop for escape, now cradled them in its midst, a symbol of triumph over the forces that sought to confine.

In the quietude of this transformative moment, James,

Marcus, Emily, and Thomas embraced the unknown, their journey symbolizing the perpetual dance between fate and free will. The pulse of the city mirrored their heartbeat, a rhythm that resonated with the harmony of newfound liberation.

As the four ventured onto the horizon, the complexities of their escape plan faded into the background, replaced by the promise of a future shaped by resilience, adaptability, and the enduring pursuit of a life unrestrained. The city, witness to their odyssey, embraced them in its urban embrace, a silent testament to the triumphant unraveling of threads that once bound them.

In this defining moment, James, Marcus, Emily, and Thomas stepped onto the canvas of their unwritten future, where the pursuit of freedom became a timeless anthem, echoing through the corridors of their shared history.

| **27** |

About the Author

Derick Chibilu is an upcoming talented author and business professional based in Houston, Texas, where he resides with his beloved wife, Alice. Known for his inspiring works, Derick holds an MBA from Capella University, a Bachelor of Business in Computer Information Systems from the University of Houston Downtown (UHD), and an Associate of Science in Business Administration from Delaware Tech.

As a born-again Christian, Derick's faith is an integral part of his life. He actively participates as a member of the North Central Assemblies of God Church in Spring, Texas, drawing strength and inspiration through fellowship with other believers. God, family, and Christian values are central themes in Derick's writing, reflecting his deep-rooted convictions.

- Derick has written extensively on various subjects such as business, leadership, personal development, and Christian spirituality. His works are highly regarded for their clarity, insight, and practicality, making them valuable resources for readers from all backgrounds. Here is a list of his books:

- Whimsical Wonders: 50 Tales of Fictional Fun
- Love As God Intended It: Faith, Hope, and Love, But the greatest of these is love.
- The Bible Storybook: 50 Exciting Stories for Kids (Volume 1)
- The Bible Storybook: 46 Parables: Tales of God's Kingdom and Our Lives (Volume 2)
- The Bible Storybook: Exploring the Transformative Power of Faith and The Miraculous Acts of Christ (Volume 3)
- Shadows of Deception: The Hidden Secrets
- Wisdom Unveiled: ~ A Collection of Pastor Kamulile's Inspirational Facebook Posts ~

"Whimsical Wonders: 50 Tales of Fictional Fun" is Derick's first foray into fiction writing and showcases his creativity and imagination. This collection of short stories has been well-received by readers of all ages.

"Love As God Intended It: Faith, Hope, and Love, But the greatest of these is love" is a Christian-themed book based on the teachings of 1 Corinthians 13. It explores the significance of love in the Christian faith.

Derick has also written "The Bible Storybook" series, which includes "50 Exciting Stories for Kids" (Volume 1), "46 Parables," and "Exploring the Transformative Power of Faith and The Miraculous Acts of Christ" (Volume 3). These books provide engaging and accessible retellings of biblical stories and teachings.

Derick Chibilu's commitment to excellence is evident in everything he does. He is a dedicated professional who takes pride in his work and is constantly seeking new ways to improve himself and his craft. Whether he is writing a new book, delivering a speech, or leading a team, Derick brings passion and enthusiasm to every endeavor.

In summary, Derick Chibilu is an inspiring author and business professional who is making a positive impact in the world. His faith, his family, and his commitment to Christian values deeply influence his life and work. Through his writing, Derick has the power to inspire and uplift readers worldwide.

****